Meg Mackintosh

and

The Mystery at Red Herring Beach

A Solve-It-Yourself Mystery

by Lucinda Landon

Secret Passage Press
Newport, Rhode Island

Books by Lucinda Landon:
Meg Mackintosh and The Case of the Missing Babe Ruth Baseball
Meg Mackintosh and The Case of the Curious Whale Watch
Meg Mackintosh and The Mystery at the Medieval Castle
Meg Mackintosh and The Mystery at Camp Creepy
Meg Mackintosh and The Mystery in the Locked Library
Meg Mackintosh and The Mystery at the Soccer Match
Meg Mackintosh and The Mystery on Main Street
Meg Mackintosh and The Stage Fright Secret

Meg Mackintosh Solves Seven American History Mysteries
American History Mysteries (Scholastic title Meg #9)
Meg Mackintosh and The Mystery at Red Herring Beach
Books illustrated by Lucinda Landon:
The Young Detective's Handbook by William Vivian Butler

About the author

Lucinda Landon has been an avid mystery fan since childhood. She lives in Newport, Rhode Island. For more clues and information about how to order books visit: www.megmackintosh.com

Copyright © 2013 by Lucinda Landon

First Edition

Library of Congress Cataloging-in-Publication Data

Landon, Lucinda.
    Meg Mackintosh and the Mystery at Red Herring Beach / a solve-it –yourself mystery / by Lucinda Landon. – 1st. ed.
    Summary: Meg and her cousin, Maxwell, search for their grandfather's missing watch while spending the afternoon on Herring Gull Beach. They find many clues and red herrings. The reader may search the pictures for key clues to solve the case along with Meg.
    (1. Mystery and detective stories. 2. Literary recreations. 3. Beach.)

Library of Congress Control Number: 2013913567

ISBN 978-1-888695-14-4

10 9 8 7 6 5 4 3 2 1

PRINTED IN THE UNITED STATES OF AMERICA

For My Animal Family:
Skye, Natty, Buddy,
Kip, Wren, Phoebe,
Oliver, Ylur, Spraekur,
Penny, Tucker, and Meadow

"Red Herring Beach! This is my absolute favorite place!" Meg Mackintosh threw her flip-flops in the air.

"Meg...CHILL" said her cousin Maxwell. He caught one of her flip-flops, then tossed it back at her.

"Don't let her kid you, Maxwell," said Gramps cheerfully. "This is really Herring Gull Beach, named after the flocks of Herring Gulls that live here."

"I know, but I like to call it 'red herring'," said Meg. "You know, the term in a mystery for clues that lead you off the track. This beach is full of clues, and I'm a detective in search of a mystery!"

Gramps rolled his eyes. "Just find us a good spot," he called to them as they ran ahead.

"This looks good," said Maxwell. He plopped down his duffle bag and spread out the beach blanket.

"Perfect!" Gramps agreed as he set up his easel. "I'm ready to paint today's masterpiece!"

"I have everything a kid needs — games, music, camera, phone," added Maxwell.

"You really don't need all that at the beach." Meg told him.

"Look at all the detecting stuff that you brought!" Max shot back.

"Oh, I guess you're right," said Meg as her notebook, pens, mystery book, and magnifying glass spilled out of her knapsack.

"I have detective devices, too," said Max.

He raised his binoculars and scanned the beach. "I'm always on the lookout for a rare bird. There are more than forty species of gulls, you know."

"Interesting fact, Maxwell," said Gramps.

"Hey, Gramps, there's your neighbor Helen. She's heading straight for us!" said Meg.

Gramps muttered under his breath. "Oh boy, 'Hurricane Helen'." Helen marched right up to Gramps. "George, why weren't you at the 'Save The Beach Birds' meeting today? We are counting on your support."

"Good afternoon, Helen," said Gramps. "Well, as you can see, I have my grandchildren visiting. You know Meg, and this is her cousin, my daughter's son, Maxwell Wing."

"Hello, Meg. Nice to meet you Maxwell, you may call me Helen, everyone does," she said briskly before turning back to Gramps. "Well, we need to protect all the birds here at Herring Gull Beach. As you know, we need your donation as soon as possible." She turned on her heel and headed back to her umbrella.

Gramps shook his head. "It's always something with Helen." He returned to his canvas.

Suddenly a football whizzed by Gramps' ear and knocked over his easel.

"Whoa!" said Gramps stumbling and then catching himself. He looked over at a man and a boy playing football nearby.

"Maybe you can move your game over a bit?" asked Gramps.

"What's the big deal?" the man replied.

"It was an accident. Wasn't it, Tucker?"

The boy looked embarrassed and nudged the man. "Come on, Dad, we can move over."

"Thanks," Gramps said and he went back to his painting.

"That was weird," Max whispered to Meg.

A little girl wandered up to Gramps' easel. "I like your picture," she told him.

"Thank you," said Gramps. "What's your name? Who's watching you?"

"I'm Sofia. My babysitter, Robin, is right over there," she told him. "I'm building a sandcastle. Do you have anything I could use to put on the top of the tower?"

Gramps shuffled through his paint box. "Here's an old key. If you put it on the top, straight up, it will look like a flag on a watchtower."

Sofia smiled. "Thanks, this is perfect." She skipped back to her castle.

"I'm ready for a swim," said Gramps.

"Me too," said Meg.

Max eyed the snack bar. "I'm kind of hungry."

"Didn't we just have lunch before we left home?" Gramps asked.

"Yeah" said Max. "But, I'm hungry again."

"Okay, that's what snack bars are for," said Gramps. He fished some money out of his pocket and handed it to Max.

"I guess I might be a little hungry, too," Meg
admitted as she pulled on her goggles. "Could you
get me a grilled cheese?"

"Come to think of it, I might need an ice tea,
cheeseburger, and French fries, when I'm done surf-
ing," Gramps joked.

Meg ran into the waves and then turned to wait
for Gramps.

"Gramps, stop!" Meg shouted. "You forgot to take
off your watch!"

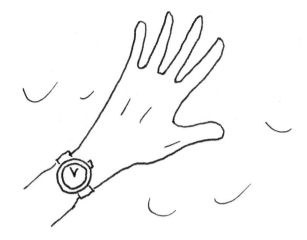

"Yikes!" said Gramps. "My good gold watch." He quickly unbuckled it and handed it to Meg.

"I'll take it back and put it in a safe place." Meg ran back to their blanket.

"Hmm," Meg thought out loud. "I'll put it under the mystery book I'm reading."

Max had stopped to look at a flock of gulls that were gathered around a waste can. He decided to do a quick drawing of one.

When he reached the snack bar, Helen was there waiting in line. She noticed Max's sketch and asked, "Are you interested in birds? That's a very nice drawing."

"Thanks" he said, "It's a Laughing Gull. I just drew it. I need my red pencil for the beak."

"Was it scavenging for food?" asked Helen.

"Yeah," said Max. "But then it flew up to the roof of the snack bar where all the gulls hang out."

"The Bird Club has permission to use the tower on the snack bar. We can view all sorts of species from there," Helen told him. "Maybe I'll go up later."

"I am actually sort of obsessed with birds" Max told Helen. "I'm president of the Ornithologist Club at my school. My last name is 'Wing' after all." He chuckled.

"Yes, of course, now I remember," said Helen. "Your grandfather told me that your family has an aviary in your apartment in the city."

"Yes, we have seven finches, three canaries, two parakeets, and one cockatoo — his name is Winston. Here is a photo of him." He showed her on his phone. "Doesn't he look like a gull with a Mohawk?"

Max layered his hot dog with mustard and relish. "I love messy food."

"Extraordinary," remarked Helen, staring at his lunch.

"Could you do me a favor?" Max asked Helen. "Could you bring Gramps' ice tea to our blanket? I don't think I can carry all of this and I'm still waiting for another sandwich."

"Happy to help," Helen replied, scooping up the paper cup. "The cover is a bit flimsy."

"Thanks," said Max. He juggled his sketchbook and tray of food and pumped ketchup into the box of French fries.

Meg and Gramps swam out to the raft where he watched her jump on and off a few times.

While Gramps floated in the waves, Meg ran back to the blanket to get her boogie board.

Max wasn't back yet, but Sofia was there poking around Gramps' paint box again.

"I was just looking for another key," Sofia explained. "For another flag for my tower."

"Sorry," called out Robin who was nearby.

"That's okay, she can't hurt anything!" called Meg as she ran back into the waves.

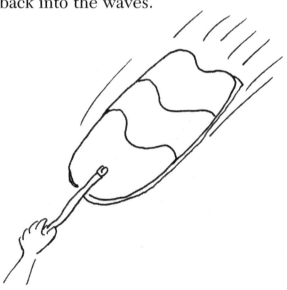

When Max returned from the snack bar, he felt the wind picking up and saw that the edges of the blanket had blown over. Some of their things had been tossed around by the wind. "Uh oh, looks like Gramps' ice tea got spilled," he said to himself. "I'll have to get him another one later."

Max spread out his second lunch. "This looks so perfect, I'm going to take a photo."

While Max was munching he noticed Meg's book lying in the sand. "Hmm, a mystery novel," he picked it up and began reading.

After a while, he was ready for a swim.

"I'M HERE!" shouted Max as he raced into the waves. The cousins took turns riding the surf on the boogie board.

After a while, Meg started shivering. "I'm getting out. I'm cold and hungry. I hope you got my grilled cheese." She stared at Max.

"Yep, and a cheeseburger and lots of fries for Gramps." Maxwell splashed her. "We'll go back later for ice cream!"

As Meg left the water, she gazed up at their blanket. "Wait a minute! What's going on up there?" She dashed through the sand.

Meg found Tucker's dad leaning over the blanket and waving his arms. Everything was a mess.

Tucker ran over. "What happened?" he asked. "I was at the snack bar."

Tucker's dad looked at Meg. "I saw some gulls over here raiding your lunch!" he told her. "So sorry I couldn't get here sooner to chase them off."

"Gee, thanks," Meg sighed, as she put on a tee shirt. She thought to herself, "Maybe he's not such a tough guy after all."

Helen approached. "Oh dear," she said. "You shouldn't leave food out like that. It's not good for the birds."

Meg rolled her eyes, "I'm sure Maxwell didn't mean to."

"A bit of chaos over here! French fries everywhere!" Meg called to Gramps and Max as they made
their way back from the water.

"I guess I should have covered up the food better,"
said Max.

"It's not that bad. At least the gulls didn't get
Gramps' cheeseburger or my grilled cheese," said Meg.

"They spilled my ice tea," said Gramps. "And my paint box is a mess!"

"Feathers and ketchup — Yuck!" said Meg. "And, Max, you left a wrapper with melted chocolate here."

"That's not mine!" Max defended himself.

"What about my watch? Meg-O, where did you put it?" Gramps' eyes scanned the blanket.

"I put it under my mystery book. It was right on the blanket." Said Meg. "But now my book is over here in the sand, and I don't see the watch!"

"It's got to be here somewhere!" Max said as they searched the area. But the watch was nowhere to be found.

"Hey, Tucker!" Max called out." "Did you see my grandfather's watch when you and your Dad were over here?"

"No, we didn't see anything. Maybe the sea gulls got it!" said Tucker. "They like to steal stuff!"

"He's right. Gulls taking things isn't that unusual," said Max.

Helen whispered to Gramps. "I'd ask that babysitter about your watch, if I were you. I saw her up here. She's always on the phone. It's suspicious."

Meg was sifting her fingers through the sand and overheard what Helen said. "Gramps, do you think someone could have taken your watch?"

Gramps had a mouthful of cheeseburger. He shook his head 'no'.

Meg reached into her detective knapsack to get her magnifying glass and began examining the scene. "It is a mystery! And I already see some clues. Max, quick take a photo!"

She opened her notebook and started jotting with her pen.

"There may be some red herrings too!" joked Max.

What clues do you see?

fries + ketchup everywhere! and feathers! ice tea spilled everything is a mess

sand in paint box - paints out candy wrapper mystery book off blanket! NO WATCH!!

"Max did you see Gramps' gold watch when you ate lunch?" Meg quizzed him, as she bit into her grilled cheese sandwich.

"No… I don't think so. But I was pretty busy eating." Max admitted.

"Let's go ask Sofia and Robin if they saw anything," Meg suggested. "Sofia was looking through Gramps' paint box when I came to get the boogie board."

Robin was on the phone. "I'll never make enough money babysitting!" she told someone, then quickly hung up.

Max and Meg asked her about the watch.

"Maybe I accidentally kicked a little sand on the blanket when I came to get Sofia, but I didn't see any watch," she told them. "Go ask Sofia. She's filling her bucket with water."

"I'm building a moat to go around my castle," Sofia told them. "When high tide comes in, the moat will fill with water."

"Very clever, Sofia," said Max. "Did you happen to see Gramps' watch when you were on the blanket? We can't find it."

Sofia shook her head. "I might have messed up a few things, but I never saw a watch."

"Well, did you drop a candy wrapper like this by any chance?" asked Meg.

"I was eating that kind of candy, but I would never, ever litter. I thought I put the wrapper in my pocket, but maybe it fell out." Her pockets were bulging with seashells and stones. "I'm sorry," Sofia blushed. "I saw someone litter today. Littering is very wrong!"

"Don't worry, Sofia," Meg told her. "It must have been an accident."

"Okay, now what do we do?" Max mumbled to Meg.

What would you do?

"Okay, let's go back and re-examine the scene," Meg replied.

She picked up her mystery book. "Hey, how did mustard get on my book?" she asked.

"Oh, I did that." Max confessed.

"You? You touched my book!" exclaimed Meg.

"Yeah, I was reading it. I like mysteries too, you know." He tried to explain.

"Well, where was the book when you picked it up?" Meg asked. "Did you see Gramps' watch underneath it?"

"I'm trying to remember…" Max paused for a moment. "I was sitting here eating, and I guess the book was just lying in the sand, because I just reached over and picked it up. It looked like the wind blew stuff around, because everything was a little messed up. I don't remember seeing the watch."

"So my book had already been knocked or blown off the blanket when you got here?" Meg asked Max. "This is an important clue."

"Meg, you could have dragged the book into the sand when you came to get the boogie board!" Max exclaimed.

"Max, you could have kicked it off when you spread out your lunch." Meg glared at him. "Is there anything else you didn't tell me?"

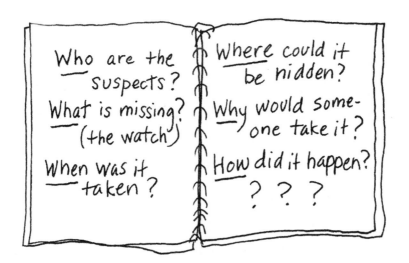

Who are the suspects?
What is missing? (the watch)
When was it taken?

Where could it be hidden?
Why would someone take it?
How did it happen? ? ? ?

What else did Max forget to tell Meg?

"Well, the ice tea was already spilled, too. So I didn't do that." Max looked down a bit guiltily. "Maybe Helen knocked it over."

"Helen was here?" Meg asked him.

"Yes, she brought Gramps' ice tea over for me." Max explained. "I couldn't carry everything and I was still waiting for our order at the snack bar. Do you think Helen would take Gramps' watch?"

"I'm making a list of suspects." Meg flipped to another page in her notebook. "A lot of people came to the blanket while Gramps and I were swimming. Any one of them could have accidentally kicked my book in the sand or maybe even stolen Gramps' watch."

"Oh, maybe there is another thing I forgot to tell you," Max realized. "I took this photo of my lunch before I ate it. But I don't see anything important in it." He showed it to her.

"Looks like a hotdog, some French fries, and a lot of ketchup." Meg shook her head. "Why is your foot in the photo like that?" she asked.

"So I could show my friends that I had a foot-long hot dog," Max laughed.

"Wait a minute. Is that the tip of the watch coming out of the sand?" Meg examined the photo more closely. "That would mean the watch was still there when you ate lunch!"

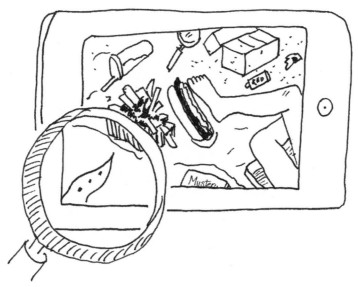

"Wow, are you sure? I don't remember seeing it."
Max was shocked.

"Okay, now we know the book and watch got
knocked off the blanket by someone, or the wind or
the gulls, but it was still here in the sand when you
ate lunch." Meg jotted in her notebook. "Now all we
have to do is figure who had the opportunity to take
it after that."

Max was exasperated. "Meg, anyone just walking
by could have taken the watch!"

Gramps spoke up. "I can't believe anyone would
take my watch. It was probably the gulls. Everyone
knows they pick up anything!"

Meg finished jotting in her notebook and handed
it to Max. "Well here are some possible suspects."

Who are the suspects?

"Ha, ha…I'm a suspect?" Said Max as he read Meg's notes.

"In a mystery, anyone can be a suspect," Meg stated.

"But, maybe Gramps is right, maybe the gulls did take it." Max scratched his head. "And if they did, I have an idea where they took it!

Where does Max think the watch *could* be?

"It could be on the roof of the snack bar," he told Meg. "That's where the gulls take everything. And I know who can take us up there — Helen!"

Helen hesitated when they asked her. "I guess it's okay, as long as we are careful. It's a bit creepy and messy."

"We don't mind creepy," said Meg.

"I like messy," agreed Max.

Helen unlocked a door at the back of the snack bar. Inside, there was a narrow spiral staircase to the top of the tower.

"I really hate to blame the birds, but it is worth a look." Helen led the way.

On the top was a small, walled platform. "It really is a turret in a castle!" said Max.

"And what a view," Meg gazed at the ocean.

"You can lean over the edge a bit and poke around with this pole," Helen handed it to Max. "It's mostly just broken shells, but maybe you'll see the watch."

"Go ahead Max, you like messy," said Meg, grinning. "Hey, the gulls even brought a French fries box up here. Maybe it's the one from our blanket!"

"This box is too old and yucky to be ours," Max decided. "Lots of junk…but no watch."

Meg gazed at the big clock mounted on the front of the tower.

"Hmm," thought Meg. "This really is a watchtower." Then she had an idea. "I'm ready go back down. Thanks for bringing us up here, Helen."

"You're welcome. I'll stay here." Helen gazed through her binoculars. "I see a piping plover!"

"Meg! What's up?" Max asked when they reached the bottom of the tower.

"I have another idea." She told him.

Now where does Meg think the watch could be?

Max followed Meg back to the beach. They found Sofia at the water's edge. "Sofia, do you have a clock on your watchtower?" Meg asked.

"Sure," said Sofia. "I have a watchtower, a moat, and a drawbridge," she said proudly. "And I even have a clock like that one!" She pointed at the clock on the snack bar watchtower. "The tide is coming in soon. I have to be sure that the water goes in to fill the moat, or the whole castle could get washed away!"

"Well come on, show us." said Max.

"This is the best castle I ever built," Sofia bragged. "Look! I drew a clock on a shell...to make it a watchtower!"

Meg gave Max a disappointed look.

"Another red herring!" said Meg. "We keep getting led off the track!"

"It's a great sandcastle, Sofia," Max told her. "The
moat is filling up just right."

"Come on, Sofia. Let's go get some ice cream."
Said Meg. "Tell Robin to come, too."

"Okay, but first I have to get something." Sofia
told them.

"Max, show me that photo you took at the blanket
after the gulls were there." Meg asked him. "Was
there a box that the French fries came in?"

Max showed her the photo. "You know, I don't
remember seeing the box when I came back from
swimming." He looked puzzled.

What is Meg thinking?

"It's just kind of strange that a French fries box is missing." Meg thought out loud.

Sofia walked up to them. "That's what I saw!" said Sofia. "I saw a guy throwing a French fries box! He threw it right through the air like a football. Remember I told you before that I saw someone littering."

"But, Sofia, you didn't tell us what he littered," said Meg. "Where were you? And when did this happen?"

"I was at my watchtower — watching!" Sofia said with a smile. "It was when the birds were all over your blanket. Now can we get the ice cream?" Sofia asked.

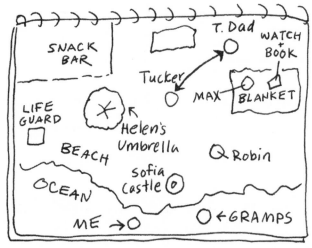

"Yes, but you guys go ahead," said Meg as she sketched in her notebook. "I have to finish drawing something."

"Max wait," Meg called out. "Before you go to the snack bar, ask Helen, Tucker, and his dad to come over to the blanket," said Meg. "Tell them we're getting ice cream for everyone to thank them for looking for Gramps' watch."

"But we didn't find it yet!" said Max.

"I know," said Meg. "I'm just trying to get some more information. And I haven't talked to everyone yet."

"Okay, I'll round up the suspects." Max muttered under his breath.

who took the watch?
?
_____
When was it taken?
?
_____

Where could it be hidden
?
_____
How did the mystery happen
?

A few minutes later, they were all gathered around the blanket.

"Could someone please explain to me what is going on?" asked Helen.

Sofia looked up at Gramps. "I'm sorry that I messed up things on your blanket. I didn't mean to litter the wrapper. I'm really sorry," she apologized. "And here's your key back."

"Oh thank you, Sofia," said Gramps. "It's okay. And keep the key for your next tower."

Sofia nodded, then looked around thoughtfully. "You're the man I saw littering," she said, turning to Tucker's dad. "Maybe you accidentally littered, like I did."

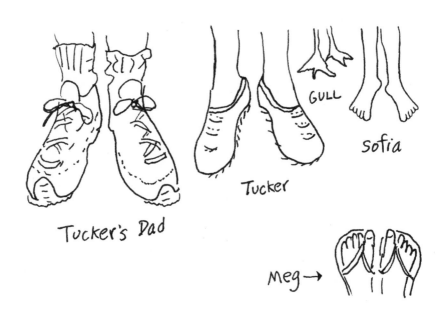

Tucker's Dad

Tucker

GULL

Sofia

Meg →

"Dad, you littered?" asked Tucker.

"It was a French fries box. I saw the stripes!" Sofia insisted. "You threw it right over there." Sophia pointed to the area of Tucker and his dad's blanket.

"But we didn't even have any French fries," exclaimed Tucker.

His dad frowned. "I was just helping clean up the mess the birds made."

Meg thought to herself. "Tucker's dad littering might explain some things."

What has Meg deduced?

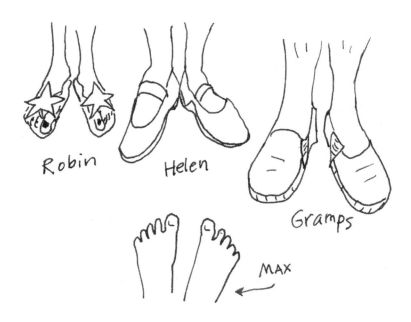

Robin

Helen

Gramps

MAX

"Why would he throw the French fries box over to his blanket?" Meg thought. "Maybe because something was inside it."

She glanced at Max and realized he had the same idea.

Max nodded at his cousin. "I'll go see if I can find the box," he said. Then he raced over to Tucker and his dad's blanket. He quickly returned with the crumpled striped box.

"Look what I found!" Max pulled the watch out of the box." Everyone was stunned.

All eyes turned to Tucker's dad.

"Dad? *You* had the watch?" Tucker was shocked."*You* took their Grandfather's watch?"

"I didn't know it was his. No one told me he lost a watch," said his dad.

"Maybe I forgot to tell you," said Tucker. "But you still shouldn't have taken it!"

"Okay, I'm sorry. I did a very stupid thing," Tucker's dad confessed. "I saw a watch in the sand. It could have been dropped by anyone!"

Tucker stared at his dad in disbelief.

"What can I do?" pleaded Tucker's dad, his face reddening. "I'll have the watch fixed if there's anything wrong with it," he offered. "I am really so very sorry. How can I make it up to you?"

Gramps gave Tucker's dad a stern look, and then he held the watch to his ear. "It's still ticking. I'm really just happy to have it back." Gramps paused. "But, I think it would be a good idea for you to volunteer to pick up litter on the beach."

Tucker's dad nodded his head. "Sure," he said quietly, "whatever you say."

"I can't believe we blamed the birds!" Helen exclaimed, then looked straight at Tucker's dad. "I have another idea what you can do!"

What could be Helen's idea?

"Since we were wrongfully blaming the gulls, you could also make a donation to the Save-The-Bird Club," suggested Helen. "Here's the address." She handed him a card.

"Sure, a donation to the Bird Club. I'll send it right away" said Tucker's dad.

"That Helen never misses a beat," Gramps muttered under his breath.

"Come on, Dad," said Tucker. "Let's get started picking up litter."

"Thank you," said Gramps. "Thanks Meg, Max, and Sofia".

"Sofia, that was good detective work from your watchtower!" Meg said.

"Thanks, but what about the ice cream?" Sofia poked Meg.

"Of course. Time for ice cream!" said Meg.

"And now the light is just right for me to finish my painting." Gramps grinned.

"Wow, we suspected everyone," said Meg.

"That's okay," agreed Max. "Like you said, every-one is a suspect in a mystery."

"Until it is solved," said Meg. "And we were really led off the track!"

"You're right!" Max agreed. "Today, on the beach there were more 'red herrings' than Herring Gulls!"

Meg grinned. "Exactly. That's why I call this place 'Red Herring Beach!'"

About the author

Lucinda Landon has always loved mysteries. She has also always loved to draw. After studying art at the Rhode Island School of Design, she illustrated *The Young Detective's Handbook*, by William Vivian Butler. That book received a special Edgar Allan Poe Award from the Mystery Writers of America and it launched Meg Mackintosh, who soon starred in her own adventures. The Meg Mackintosh Mystery series is now ten books strong, all published by Secret Passage Press. Meg and her brother Peter also appear in *American History Mysteries*, which Ms. Landon wrote and illustrated. Lucinda Landon lives in Newport, Rhode Island.

Photograph by Ned Landon

Lucinda Landon at about the same age as Meg Mackintosh.

Learn more about Meg Mackintosh at:
www.megmackintosh.com